For Amy, the seal,
with love—A. D.
To Frances—V. C.

Text © 2007 Alan Durant

Illustrations © 2007 Vanessa Cabban

First U.S. edition 2007

Library of Congress Cataloging-in-Publication Data is available.

Library of Congress Catalog Card Number 2006930962

ISBN 978-0-7636-3442-1

10 9 8 7 6 5 4 3 2 1

Printed in China

This book was typeset in Palatino, with hand-lettering by Helena Blakeway. The illustrations were done in watercolor.

Candlewick Press, 2067 Massachusetts Avenue, Cambridge, Massachusetts 02140

visit us at www.candlewick.com

Dear Mermaid

Alan Durant

illustrated by Vanessa Cabban

CANDLEWICK PRESS

CAMBRIDGE, MASSACHUSETTS

One summer, Holly stayed with her family in a cabin
by the sea. On the first day, she found something on the beach.
Her mom said it was a mermaid's purse.
I'd better give it back, thought Holly. So that evening she left the purse
on the beach, and she wrote a note in the sand.

Dear Mermaid,
Is this your purse?
I found it in the sand.
What's it like being a mermaid?
Is it fun living under the sea?
PLEASE write back.
Love, HOLLY

The next morning, Holly's note had been washed away by the sea. But the mermaid's purse was still there—and there was a letter inside!

Holly

"That letter smells fishy," said her little brother, Billy. "It's from a mermaid princess!" said Holly.

Holly was delighted with her letter.
She read it over and over.
She really wanted to find the mermaid's
lost key, so she searched
the beach all day.

Later, she wrote another note to Princess Kora and left it in the mermaid's purse on the beach.

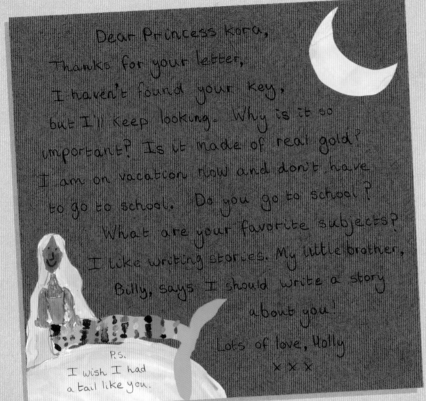

Dear Princess Kora,
Thanks for your letter,
I haven't found your key,
but I'll keep looking. Why is it so
important? Is it made of real gold?
I am on vacation now and don't have
to go to school. Do you go to school?
What are your favorite subjects?
I like writing stories. My little brother,
Billy, says I should write a story
about you!
Lots of love, Holly
x x x

P.S.
I wish I had
a tail like you.

That night the mermaid swam up from under the sea. She read Holly's note and sighed. Then she left a reply.

The next day, Holly ran to the beach
and opened the mermaid's purse.
She read the letter inside.

Holly loved the letter—
and the book. She showed
it to Billy. He loved it, too.
"Imagine being taught
by a lobster,"
said Holly
with a laugh.

All that day, Holly and Billy played on the beach. Holly didn't find the mermaid's key, but she collected lots of beautiful shells. She put a few in the mermaid's purse with her note.

Dear Princess Kora,

Thanks so much for the book. I'm afraid I haven't found your key yet, but I'll keep looking.

Please tell me some more about the Mer Festival.

Lots of love, Holly x

P.S. Aren't sea horses too small to ride?

P.P.S. I'm going on a pony ride!

The next day, after breakfast,
Holly ran down to the beach
and picked up the mermaid's purse.

Holly loved her picture frame. She put
a photo of herself inside and stood it on her bedside table
next to her shells. Later, as she trotted across the sand
on her pony ride, she thought of Princess Kora
galloping through the ocean
with her sea horses.

In the afternoon, it rained and Holly had to stay inside. She wrote another note to Princess Kora.

Dear Princess Kora,

Sorry, still no sign of your key.

My pony ride was fun but slow—riding a sea horse must be much more exciting! Billy and I played Chutes and Ladders and tic-tac-toe today. Do you like playing games?

Thanks for the lovely picture frame.

The Mer festival sounds wonderful. I'd be so excited if I were you.

Why don't you tell your mother about the key?

I'm sure she won't be as angry as you think.

Lots of love,

Holly x

That night, when the moon was bright,
the mermaid swam up once more
from her home under the sea.
She read Holly's note
and left a reply.

The next day was the last day of Holly's vacation. She went down to the beach and found Princess Kora's letter.

Holly played the mermaid's game with Billy. Then they played on the beach and in the sea. Holly imagined her friend all dressed up for the Mer Festival. "I wish I could find that little golden key," she said wistfully.

After lunch, Holly looked at her special shells.
She held her favorite shell up to her ear . . .
and something fell out. It was small
and golden—the missing key!
Quickly, Holly wrote to the mermaid.

Dear Princess kora,
   I've found your key!
It was in one of my shells! I hope you have
fun at the Mer Festival. Your outfit sounds
amazing. The game you gave me is
really good. I'll play it lots and will think
of you. I'm going home tomorrow, so this
will be my last note. Thanks for everything.
   Lots of love,
   Your on-the-land friend,
   Holly xx

Holly put the note and the key
in the purse and ran to the beach.

That night Holly dreamed
about Princess Kora and the Mer Festival.
The mermaid was singing a beautiful song.

Holly opened her eyes,
and she could still hear the singing.
She got out of bed and went to the window.
There was Princess Kora! Holly waved.
The mermaid smiled and waved back.
"Thank you, Holly!"
she called. Then she
dived beneath
the waves.